A CIA Fox

Written and Illustrated by

Lauren Duke

ISBN: 0989084647
ISBN-13: 978-0989084642

CHAPTER 1

The whip hit my back, leaving a long bleeding gash as it tore through my shirt and dug into me. My arms, tied high above my head by leather straps to a horizontal pole, were just beginning to ache. My legs, toes barely touching the ground, couldn't carry my weight anymore. My knees buckled, adding more stress to my arms. I groaned in terrible agony. The black wolf chuckled menacingly as he hit me again. This agent of P.A.W. had no compassion. Groaning, I felt the blood from the gashes oozing down my back. I heard the whip slicing through the air. My muscles tensed as they prepared for the stinging impact. But, the blow never came. There was no third lash. Then, I heard someone groan. With great effort, I turned my head so I could see where the groan had come from. I looked into the expressionless

1

eyes of Jayden. Giving me a small smile, he turned to the wolf.

"I'll take it from here, Coal," he said, basically ripping the whip from the wolf's grasp.

Keeping his eyes cast down, Coal hurriedly left the dark damp torture chamber. My head hung limply from lack of strength. I felt the straps being loosened from around my swollen wrists, strong arms wrapped around my chest to support me and a calm voice whispered in my ear.

"It's okay, Scarlet. I gotcha, I gotcha."

My vision began to cloud, my eyes closed and that's when I jerked awake. Sighing in relief, I realized it had all been a dream. Lying back down, I closed my eyes and fell back into a sweet sleep.

∞

Six months later

I walked into the CIA headquarters and up to the pretty little Pomeranian at the front desk.

"Hey, Penelope!" I said, propping my elbows up on the solid white desk.

The bright blue ribbon on the top of her head bobbed up and down when she looked up.

"Hey, Carter! What can I do for you?" she asked, smiling at me, then turned her attention back to her computer.

"Could you tell me if Peter is here?"

"Give me one second and I'll check," she said, and then began to type away on her keyboard. "Yeah, he's here."

I gave her a quick nod. "Thanks, Penelope."

I walked towards the elevator and pressed the little square button. Suddenly, I felt something brush my shoulder. Turning around to look, I gasped in surprise.

"Silver!" I exclaimed, playfully punching the tall grey wolf in the arm when I saw him grinning.

"What? Can't take a little scare?" he asked, pushing me into the elevator when it opened.

"Not when it's played on *me!*"

"Aw, that's sad, Savine."

"Oh, quit," I said, stepping out of the elevator when it opened. I raised an eyebrow and cocked my head. "By the way, I thought today was your day off?"

"It is, but Peter wanted to talk to me."

My heart skipped a beat. Why would Peter want to talk to Silver? Was Peter having Silver follow me? Or worse, was *Enigma* having Silver follow me? I frowned at myself. There I went again with my trust issues. I frowned at Silver, but a smile played on my mouth.

"I wonder why..." I murmured, looking ahead of us.

We rounded the corner of the hallway that led to Peter's office. That's when I saw him. A coal black fox with stone cold frosty blue eyes leaning on the wall next to Peter's door. He had his arms crossed, dressed in a slick black leather jacket with a red T-shirt, jeans, and he was watching me. I froze in place. I breathed in short, quick intakes. My jaw slackened and my eyes widened in shock. It couldn't be! I felt a heavy paw on my shoulder, which made me tear my gaze away from the mysterious fox. Silver looked at me, concern resting deep within his blue eyes.

"Are you okay, Savine?" he asked, his face riddled with concern.

"What? Oh, yeah, sure. I'm okay," I said quickly, turning back to look at the fox.

He was gone! I quickly walked over to Peter's door, looked up and down the hallway, hoping to spot him. Unfortunately, the hallway was too crowded. I burst into Peter's office, looking wildly about, half expecting the fox to be in there. Not a chance. Peter looked up calmly from his desk.

"There you are, Savine!"

Marching over to his desk where he was sitting, I looked him straight in the eyes. "Was there a black fox in here?"

Peter furrowed his brow at me and shook his furry grey head slightly. "No...why? What's so important about a black fox?"

With a heavy sigh, I plopped down into the nearest seat.

"Nothing...I just thought I saw someone that I knew."

The large grey wolf got a playful smile on his face. "You've said that before."

Rolling my eyes, I glanced up at him. "Okay, okay...I know I have. You said you had news about Ivan."

"Yes, I do. You're not going to like this. My sources tell me that he's escaped prison."

I felt the hackles on my neck rise. "Great. Just great. Now we're going to have to find him. *Again*."

Groaning, I covered my face with my paws and shook my head. Rising from his chair, Peter ushered me out the door.

"Oh, you know you love it, Savine," he said, a paw on the doorknob.

"Yeah, I sure do. Well, see you later," I called back to him as I made my way back to the elevator.

I almost stopped in my tracks again. Where had Silver gone? I shook my head, frowning. I had to stop being so suspicious. He was probably just talking to another agent. I got into the elevator when it opened, while my mind was wandering. After I said goodbye to Penelope, I left the lobby and walked out of the CIA building. Then, I located my brand new purple Camry. Unlocking it, I grabbed the handle and pulled. The door was almost all the way open when a black and tan paw slammed against it, making it close with a loud bang, causing me to jump.

Turning angrily, I growled, "What was tha-" I froze.

Lucas O'Meara stood before me. Grinning menacingly at me, he quickly grabbed my arm.

"Hello, Agent Savine. Nice to see you again."

I tried to pull away from him, but he gripped my arm tighter. "Don't struggle. It'll only make things harder for you."

I glared at him, my tail ridged with anger. "What do you want, Lucas?"

The Rottweiler licked his lips and leaned in close to me. "What do I want? It's not what I want, it's what Ivan wants. I expect you remember Ivan, right?"

7

My ears flattened against my head. "So, what does Ivan want with me?"

Lucas chuckled sinisterly at me. "Well, you put him in jail. You ruined his plans. Every bounty hunter has heard about the price on your head. Ivan wants you alive and in his grasp. You, Scarlet Savine, are the most wanted canine. What did you expect? A bouquet of roses?"

"Don't push it, Lucas. You might have a strong grip, but I have a loud scream. You want me to co-operate? Fine. I'll do what you ask. But if you say one more sarcastic word, I'll make sure my paw hits you in the mouth."

Lucas grinned at me. "I'd like to see you try."

I threw my arm back, but before I could take a swing at him, he shoved me into the backseat of my car. Opening the driver's door, Lucas climbed into my car. Closing the door softly, he started the engine. I instantly sat up and started opening my door when he locked it. I reached for him, but he pressed on the gas pedal and the car shot forward with a lurch, sending me back into the seat. Reluctantly, I relaxed and glared at the back of his head.

"I do hope you know that my friends will be

looking for me," I said, irritated that I had allowed myself to be foxnapped.

"Oh, you call them your friends? Rumor has it you don't even trust them," he said sarcastically, grinning at me in the rearview mirror.

"I may not trust them, but at least they care about me."

"*Care* about you? You think they *care* about you? Haha, that's a good one, Savine! They *care* about you. Is that what you really think?"

Rolling my eyes, I looked out the window. "Yes, that's what I think."

"Well, let me tell you something. Your *friends*, as you call them, don't care about you. All they care about is who your brother is."

I furrowed my brow. "My brother? That makes no sense, we haven't heard from him in years!"

Lucas looked into my eyes. "You really don't know anything, do you?"

I leaned forward in my seat. "Tell me, what does my brother have to do with this?"

Chuckling, the Rottweiler looked ahead at the road. "Wow, Savine. Here, I thought you knew everything there was to know about your family, but I guess I was wrong."

Growling, I looked at him in the mirror. "Lucas O'Meara, tell me what my brother has to do with this!"

"Hey, do you remember what Enigma told you the first day y'all met? 'Answers will come to your questions in time.' I think you'd better start listening to him more often."

I flopped back in my seat with a heavy sigh, knowing any further questions would be met with silence. Frowning, my mind became a whirlwind of questions. Why did Ivan need me? When did he find out that I wasn't dead? Where was he taking me? Why does Lucas always pop up in my work? How did he find me? And what were my friends going to do when they found out I was missing?

CHAPTER 2

"What do you mean you can't find her?!" Enigma
snarled angrily at Silver, clinching his paws.

The lighter grey wolf raised his paws up next to his
head, innocently. "Don't yell! I just said I didn't know
where she was!"

Enigma paced up and down the empty hallway. "Do
you have *any* idea how much she means in terms of
winning the war against P.A.W.?!"

Silver crossed his arms and put all his weight on
one footpaw. "Is that *all* you care about?"

The darker grey wolf stopped dead in his tracks,
slowly turned and glared at Silver with dark blue eyes.

"No, of course not. But, she is important to the fact
that she is the *key* in winning the war!"

Silver, looking down at the ground, sighed, "I
know, I know. You don't have to keep telling me."

"Have you tried her cell?"

"Yes, three times already."

"Try it again."

Silver grabbed his phone from his pants pocket and punched in Scarlets number. It rang for a few moments, then...

"*Hello, this is Savine,*" came a familiar voice.

"Savine, you-"

"*Sorry I can't answer the phone right now, I must be busy. Leave a message at the tone.*"

Groaning, Silver hung up the phone. "Her voicemail. Again."

Enigma ran a paw through his fur and continued to pace. "Great! Just great! Where did she run off to?"

"Maybe she didn't go voluntarily." Silver stopped dead in his tracks.

"What'd you mean?"

"Maybe she was forced to go somewhere."

"You mean, like, foxnapped?"

"Something like that. Yeah, why not?"

Enigma paused for a second. "Get the security footage of the parking lot, elevators, everywhere."

"Got it!" Silver took off down the hallway.

Sighing in frustration, Enigma turned to the creamy

colored wall and rested his forehead on it. "Where did you take off to, Savine? Where?"

"Did I hear the name Savine?" came a deep, silky smooth voice from behind him.

Enigma whirled around to come snout to snout with the black fox. He gazed straight into the frosty blue eyes that stared unblinking back at him.

"Yes, you did. What do you want?" Enigma asked, frowning ever so slightly.

"Listen carefully. If you ever want to see Scarlet again, you're going to have to do as I say. Got it?"

Enigma nodded hastily. "I'll do anything. What's your name?"

The fox gave Enigma a chilling smile. "They call me Jayden."

CHAPTER 3

I stared out the window with a heavy sigh and crossed my arms. Lucas looked back at me.

"What? Not enjoying your little ride?" he asked, grinning.

I glared at him out of the corner of my eye. "No, not very much. I would much rather know *where* I'm going."

Chuckling, he pulled the car over onto a dirt road. I was jarred around by all the bumps, gouges and deep valleys in it. Rocks flew from under the tires as they spun.

"Couldn't you have chosen a smoo-*ooff*-ther road?" I asked, trying to brace myself.

Lucas seemed unaffected by the road, continuing to smile. "Well, if it was a smoother road, more animals would come down it. The bumps and dips act as a deterrent. Ivan doesn't want animals coming down and seeing what's happening."

Whump! My head hit the window. I groaned and rubbed it with the pad of my paw. "Ow...I can see why no one comes down here...Ivan did pick a good road..."

Lucas chuckled and I looked back out my window. It was getting darker. The trees and shrubs were getting thicker; the road curved around them and the setting sun was peeking through the branches of the trees. I felt a shiver go down my back. Then, I frowned at myself. There was no reason to be afraid. Just a creepy...eerie...strange curving road...with trees and bushes so thick you can't see through them. Yeah, there's no reason to be afraid. I let out a deep breath. *Get it together, Scarlet*, I told myself. Now, the sun had disappeared and the moon was rising high into the silent night sky. Quite suddenly, the trees stopped flying by my window and the road widened. That's when I saw a huge valley. In the full moon's light, I could see the towering white building. Strobe lights on all four corners, an eight-foot-tall fence with barbed wire on the top surrounded the perimeter. Two towers placed on opposite sides of the metal gate guarded the entrance. I froze. What was Ivan planning? What was going on in his hardheaded mind? The car rolled to a stop as we neared the gate. A lanky Doberman Pinscher dressed in military uniform came out of a small building next to the gate and walked over to Lucas' rolled down window.

"I.D.," he said, in a high pitched, squeaky voice.

Lucas handed him an I.D. slip. After comparing the photo to Lucas, the Doberman handed the I.D. back to the Rottweiler. Then, it hit me. Lucas didn't have his accent any more. Frowning, I gazed curiously at him.

"Lucas, where'd your accent go?"

"That was fake. Ivan wanted to see how you reacted in certain situations. Like the first case you had with Silver."

I immediately stiffened and felt the fur on my neck stand up. "You mean to tell me Ivan knew about me from the very beginning?"

"Yeah, that's what I mean."

"So, the murder...er...burglary was a setup?"

"That's what I'm telling you," he said, applying pressure to the brake.

My car rolled to a stop in front of the building. Getting out and coming around to my door, Lucas pulled me out of the car. I ripped myself out of his grasp and glared at him.

"Okay, listen Lucas, I'm not going to try and get away. I'm too curious."

"Curiosity killed the fox, eh?"

Grinning at me, he let me walk beside him into the P.A.W. headquarters. Through sliding doors and metal detectors we walked before arriving in the main lobby. Canines and felines, badgers and wolverines, animals of every kind walked in and out of the maze of hallways that connected to the lobby.

"Well, well! If it isn't Scarlet Savine!" said a loud, clear as a bell voice, causing everyone stop and stare at me.

I felt the heat rise to my cheeks as I felt their watchful eyes on me. A Karelian bear dog strode up out of the crowd. Instantly bristling, I felt my lips curling back into a small snarl that quickly disappeared.

"Cody!" I basically hissed between gritted teeth.

The black and white splotched dog only grinned at me, his tail slowly swaying back and forth.

"Glad to see me?"

"Hardly."

The hackles rose on my back and my legs tensed as Cody strode closer to me, chuckling. Walking around me in a small circle, he sized me up. Standing almost snout to snout with me, he looked me right in the eyes.

"You haven't changed a bit, Savine," he said, giving me a lopsided smile. Leaning in close to where his snout was near my ear, he whispered, "I heard about what you did to Sam."

A deep growl emitted from my chest and my lips edged back slowly, revealing two sharp canines. "What about him? I never got to see the runt killed, if he was."

Cody looked around, a huge grin plastered on his face, then he looked back at me. "So, you don't know what happened?"

I narrowed my eyes at him and tilted my head back slightly. "No, I don't. What happened to that little backstabber?"

"That room you threw him into contained an eel. Sort of a pet project of Ivan's. Sam became lunch for the overgrown worm."

I raised a paw to my throat and rubbed it. "Wow...that must've been gruesome..."

Cody gave me another lopsided smile and turned around, motioning for me to follow him. "Come on, Savine. Ivan isn't here right now, so we're going to have to give you a room or something..."

Taking in a deep breath, I held it, waiting for him to

continue.

"What would you prefer?"

I hesitated before answering him. "A room."

I started following him, then his head turned slightly so he could look at me, another one of his lopsided smiles on his face.

"Nice try. A cell for you."

"Why?" I asked, sarcastically.

"Because."

"Because, why?"

Cody looked back at me, giving me an annoyed look. "You sure do ask a lot of questions."

"Hey, I'm a curious fox."

Cody looked away, ignoring me. A black wolf quickly walked up to Cody.

"Sir, the cell isn't ready for her yet," he said, nodding in my direction.

The Karelian bear dog nodded. "Okay, Coal. Do we have any other cells that are not in use or that have not been...bloodstained?"

The black wolf smiled menacingly and snickered. "Maybe. I'll go look."

Swallowing hard, I stood next to Cody. "B-bloodstained?" I stammered.

He gave me another one of his lopsided smiles. "Didn't you know? Coal is our torturer. We needed information from the last canine that occupied your cell, so we brought Coal in to do the job."

I fearfully watched the monstrous figure of the wolf disappearing down the hall. I wrinkled my nose at my thoughts and looked at Cody.

"Well, then, lead me to my cell."

Cody began to walk again and I followed him, keeping up with his pace. After a short walk, we arrived at a white door. Cody opened it and pushed me in. My paws couldn't get traction on the white tile floor, so I slid across it until my leg hit a neatly made bed. The door behind me closed with a click. With a heavy sigh, I flopped down on the bed. I had made a horrible mistake in letting Lucas bring me here. Covering my face with my paws, I heaved a sigh, not bothering to look at the room. All I could think about was that I needed to trust that my friends would look for me.

CHAPTER 4

Enigma sat uncomfortably in the black SUV next to the silent black fox called Jayden. The wolf cleared his throat and looked at the fox.

"So...where're we going?"

No response.

"Do you have a plan?"

A single ear twitched.

"Do you know where she is?"

There was an irritated sigh; the blue eyes looked skyward as if searching for help, then Jayden finally spoke.

"You ask a lot of questions, Kyle," he said, his once calm voice had an edge to it now.

"Yeah, I do, especially when mysterious black foxes suddenly appear from nowhere saying they can help me find Savine. And how do you know my name?"

Jayden looked patiently at Enigma, then turned his attention back to the road.

"Answers will come to your questions in time. But, first, we have to go get some animals."

Enigma cocked his head and raised an eyebrow. "May I ask who?"

Jayden gave him a, 'Seriously? It's obvious,' look. Enigma curled his lips in disgust, glaring severely at the fox.

"That's it, you cheeky pup, I'm not going to take any more sarcastic lip from you, understand?"

Rolling his eyes, Jayden looked back at the road. "Yeah, yeah. You know the animals I'm talking about."

Furrowing his brow, Enigma looked at the strange fox.

"Sasha and Jack?"

Jayden nodded.

"Will and Silver?"

The black fox laughed quietly. "Bravo, Kyle, bravo. You're a genius!"

The deep blue eyes of Enigma were sending daggers of hate towards Jayden as they pulled into the driveway of the familiar white house. The stone cold eyes of the fox stared unblinking at the door. A long drawn out breath escaped him. Enigma looked at him as he climbed out of the SUV.

"Something wrong?" he asked, raising an eyebrow.

"What? Oh, no," Jayden said quickly, hurriedly getting out of the car.

"Good."

The pair made their way up to the door. Grabbing the doorknob, Enigma opened the door, it squeaked loudly as it swung on its hinges. A tall, lanky dingo immediately poked his around the corner.

"Enigma! Hey! Who's the fox?"

A grey fox rounded the corner and saw Enigma first. "Enigma! What're yo-?"

Sasha stopped dead in her tracks when she saw the black fox.

"Jayden?" she asked, her eyes widening.

The strange canine shuffled his footpaws nervously and wouldn't meet her gaze.

"Hello, Sasha...long time no see..."

Suddenly, Jayden felt arms wrap around him in a tight embrace. Enigma's eyes widened when he saw the two foxes hugging, then he frowned.

"Sasha, who is this guy?"

Finally letting Jayden go, Sasha grinned like a

mischievous kit.

"I'll explain later...oh, Jayden! I missed you!" she went on, her paws all over Jayden's head, running them through his fur. "Oh! I have to tell Scarlet!"

Jayden grabbed Sasha's paws before she had a chance to grab her phone. He gazed into her amber eyes with his frosty blue ones.

"That's why I'm here. Scarlet has been taken by Lucas O'Meara."

"What?!"

"I'll need all the help I can get, though, if we're going to get her back."

Sasha nodded her head dutifully. "Okay, what do you need?"

"I need Jack. Where is he?"

"At the store...he should be back any minute, though."

"Okay, good."

Enigma stepped in. "If we're going to do this, I'm helping."

"Me, too," Will said, coming up beside Enigma.

Jayden smiled at them. "Okay. Now, here's what we're going to do..."

Outside, the wind played with the falling leaves of

autumn, rustled the drying grass and ruffled the black fur of the cat. Her green eyes watched the movement in the house. Her lips curled into a sinister smile. This is what she'd been trained for. Spying.

CHAPTER 5

I sat on the bed of my cell, staring blankly at the wall. Why did I let myself get dragged into this? I rolled my eyes. Because, I'm as curious as a cat. Maybe even more so than a cat. The cell door opened and Cody peered in.

"Come on, Savine, Ivan's back," he said, motioning for me to follow.

Standing, I let him lead me back through the maze of halls to double doors. Grabbing both doorknobs, the Karelian bear dog swung the doors open. I took a step into the office and looked at the opposite end of it. Behind a desk, that looked like an exact replica of the one back in Germany, sat the magnificent wolverine, Ivan O'Mealo. He stared straight at me as I walked in. The wolverine smiled, exposing a row of shiny sharp teeth.

"Scarlet Savine, a CIA fox, da? You made an improvement for who you work for."

The hackles rose along my spine. "Maybe...depends on how you look at it."

"Please, sit," he requested, pointing a long curving claw at a chair.

I edged cautiously towards the leather cushioned chair. "So, what's happened with you since we last met?"

Ivan's eyes immediately narrowed. "You made a grave mistake when you tried to stop the war. You made me your enemy, Savine, da? Then, you killed Sam, my strong right paw. You will pay heavily for your crimes!"

I sat down quickly. "I killed Sam? Rumor has it your own eel ate him!"

The lips of Ivan's snout pulled back into a hideous snarl. "Guards, take Savine to her cell! Tell Coal he has his duty to perform!"

Two guards grabbed me by my arms, hauled me upright and led me back to my cell. They shoved me in and I slid on the floor until my leg hit the bed. Fear raised its ugly head in my chest when I thought about what Ivan had said. What *was* Coal's job around here again? Then, it came to me. He was the torturer! Great. That big black brute looked strong. He could probably do some damage. Unexpectedly, the door to my cell opened and hit the wall with a slam. Coal stood in the doorway like some dark villain straight out of a comic book. Behind him stood a light brown fox with a buttery creamy stripe running down his spine and faded as it spread out across his back. The hazel eyes, flecked beautifully with green, held my gaze for a second. I knew I had seen him somewhere, I just couldn't place it. Coal stared at me with his almond shaped chocolate brown eyes.

"Follow me," he said, holding an outstretched arm to me.

I slowly walked towards him. I felt his paw on my back as I walked past him. It sent a cold shiver down my spine. Coal and his little friend guided me down the long empty hall. The clicking of our claws echoed down it, my ears twitched at every little sound. The black wolf stopped me in front of a wide metal door. I swallowed hard. What was behind that door? His black paw slowly reached out to grab the doorknob. He slowly twisted it. I could hear my heart beating in my head. The door creaked as it swung on its hinges. Coal pushed me into the pitch black room, then switched on the light. A table with scalpels, scissors, and knives sat beside a bloodstained bed with leather straps. Only a few feet away from that, two poles stuck vertically in the ground with another pole attached to the top of them. Dangling down from the top pole were two leather straps. Right beside this element of torture was a rack with different whips. There were other torturing objects in the room, but are far too horrifying to write down. I heard a sinister low laugh from behind me. I turned around slowly. Coal and his friend stood in the doorway. The muscular wolf stepped into the room as I took a step back. The familiar looking fox followed.

"So, you know what I do. What do you think?"

I snorted. "Think? I think you're a sicko!"

Coal chuckled menacingly, slowly bobbing his head up and down. "That's what most animals think. So, what'll I do to you?" He paused, then looked at the fox. "Come here, Gideon, I need your help."

Gideon walked over to him, a bored look on his face. "Yeah? What do you need?"

"Tie Miss Savine to the poles."

The light brown fox looked at me with his soft hazel eyes, flecked wonderfully with green. "Why do we have to hurt her? What did she do?"

Coal grabbed the fox's ear between his claws and

wrenched it, making Gideon yelp in pain.

"You're paid to do a job, not to think!"

Gideon tore himself from Coal's grasp and glared at him, taking deep breaths.

"Yes, sir," he said bitterly and walked over to me.

I looked at the fox's face as he tied my paws in the leather straps. Where had I seen him before? Then, it struck me.

"Gideon?" My eyes widened in astonishment.

The light brown fox winked roguishly at me.

"Hey, Scarlet, how ya doin'?" he whispered.

I stared at him, not believing that he stood before me.

"But, but! We lost you in the fire!"

Gideon put a paw over my mouth. "Not so loud! I'm undercover! Sorry for what Coal's about to do to you, but...I can't be exposed. Not yet, at least."

Backing away from me, Gideon nodded.

"She's ready, Coal!"

There was a whizzing sound in the air, then a sharp searing pain coursed across my back. I howled in agony, my entire body tensing. Coal chuckled, then the same whizzing sound struck my ears. The same pain sliced across my back. I screamed, in response to the agonizing pain. Each time the monstrous wolf hit me with the whip, it tore my shirt, ripping my skin. I could feel blood running down from the gashes. With watery eyes, I looked up at Gideon. He flinched each time Coal hit me. The long leather whip hit my back again, leaving behind another gash. A tear slipped down my face. Each time it hit me, it reopened scars from my first encounter with Ivan. I don't know how long I was in that torture chamber, but when the wolf stopped for the day, I couldn't feel my back. My head was dizzy, my vision clouded, then my head dropped from lack of strength. The last thing I remembered was Gideon helping me out of the straps.

CHAPTER 6

Gem heard a knock on her door, so she gracefully got up from her chair and went to open it. The door slowly opened and the black cat peered around it. A thick Rottweiler sneered at her, his ears laid flat against his head.

"Ivan said you had something important to tell him," he said, pushing against the door, so he could get into Gem's house.

Her thick black tail twitched angrily as her keen green eyes watched Lucas.

"About time you showed up, O'Meara," she said, walking over to a stool near her kitchen table.

The tan lips of the Rottweiler curled as he snarled at her, but he followed her into the kitchen.

"Cut to the point, cat," his voice dripped with hatred.

The sleek cat sat down in an airy manner. A low purr erupting from her throat.

"Is someone in a rush today?"

Lucas' muscles tensed, he narrowed his eyes.

"What did you have to say, Gem?"

Four shiny, thin black claws appeared from one of Gem's soft elegant paws. She flexed her paw, liking the sound her claws made against the counter top.

"The black fox has met Sasha. They're planning to find Scarlet," she said softly, clinching her paw.

Lucas looked at her curiously. "How do you know this?"

One of her ears twitched impatiently, her pupils shrunk into two thin slits, her tail twitched back and forth.

"Do you doubt my word?"

The Rottweiler gave her a cocky lopsided grin and shifted his weight.

"I only asked a question. How did you find out this information?"

Black claws tapped on the countertop as Gem pondered answering him. A deep heavy sigh escaped her and she flattened her ears. Gem looked at him with slanted eyes.

"I was trained to be a spy. How did I get this information? I spied on them. Does this satisfy you?"

Lucas gave her a content smile. "Total satisfaction."

The black cat slid out of her chair like water.

"Then, let me lead you to the door."

Lucas gave her a disappointed look. "Aw, that's mean. You don't like my company?" he said, in a mocking tone.

Gem gave the irritable canine a fake smile. "Would you?"

She opened the door with a jerk. Lucas took a step out of the house and the door slammed behind him. A huge grin slowly crept up his face. Pulling the hood of his jacket over his head, he walked down the concrete steps of her porch.

"No, I wouldn't like my company. I'm just too smart for some animals!"

Lucas walked down the sidewalk and caught up with a dirty blond fox with a brown undercoat. The fox's hazel eyes, flecked with green, sparkled as he smiled at the Rottweiler.

"Did you get what you needed?" he asked, sticking his paws into his black leather jacket, walking alongside Lucas.

The dark brown eyes of the dog barely looked at the fox as he replied, "Yeah, I got it, Amos."

Chuckling, Amos looked at Lucas. "So, what's the history between you and that cat?"

A warning growl emitted from deep within Lucas' chest. "None of your business! If you keep asking questions, though, it will be!"

Amos bobbed his head up and down. "Okay, okay! Fair enough! Boy, you sure are secretive."

CHAPTER 7

Enigma rolled his eyes at the sound of Jayden and Sasha yammering away in the back of his car. They had picked up Silver at the CIA building. He had been worried that I might be in serious trouble. The grey wolf had been ready to do anything to help. Now, a heavy irritated sigh escaped him. Enigma chuckled dryly. The two wolves in the front of the car shared a secret glance at each other. Both were thinking the other same thing. When were those two foxes going to stop chattering like a couple of squirrels?

"Where did you find that wolf, Enigma? I've been trying to for years," Jayden was saying.

With one look in the rearview mirror, Enigma tried to put an end to the black fox's chatter. Silver let out a sigh of relief when they stopped.

"Silence, at last!"

A grey paw shot out of the back seat and hit him on the back of the head.

Silver flinched and looked back at Sasha. "What was that for?!"

There was some giggling before Sasha could reply.

"For saying that!"

Enigma snickered and glanced at Silver. "You have to admit, that was funny."

Eyes widening, Silver looked at Enigma in disbelief.

"Oh, so, you're taking their side, eh? Over your own kind! Wow!"

A black paw hit him in the head this time. Turning around in his seat, Silver glared at the two foxes.

"Do it one more time and you're going to get it!"

Jayden snickered and tilted his head back slightly. "Get what?"

Enigma chuckled again. "All right, settle down. Let's focus on the situation at paw, okay?"

Jayden and Sasha forced themselves to keep straight faces.

"Right!"

Enigma looked in the rearview mirror at the blue eyed fox. "Okay, Mr. Jayden, where to?"

"Well, I'd have to drive, if you want to find her."

Heaving a sigh, Enigma pulled the car onto the side of the road. Exchanging seats, Jayden now drove the SUV. Enigma sat next to the bubbling-with-excitement Sasha. The grey fox just couldn't sit still! She kept touching him, talking non-stop, and laughing loudly. He leaned forward in his seat, trying to look Silver in the eye.

"Want to trade spots?"

Silver chuckled and shook his head. "No, thanks! You didn't stick up for me, so I'm not sticking up for you!"

"Oh, gee, thanks...I feel so loved..."

Jayden rolled his eyes and looked at Sasha in the rearview mirror. "Do they always act like this?"

"No...this is the first time."

Enigma saw the black head bob up and down. "Huh!"

"So, Jayden, where're you taking us?" Enigma asked, leaning back in his seat.

The blue eyes flickered up to meet his gaze, then moved back down. White teeth flashed in the light cast by the setting sun as he spoke.

"Friends, be prepared to go into the heart of P.A.W.!"

CHAPTER 8

There was a pounding sensation in my head, like someone was beating drums. My eyelids slowly opened, only to have a light blind me. Holding up a black paw to block it out, I painfully sat up. Where was I? Then, I remembered. In a cell. In P.A.W. headquarters and I had been beaten. I squinted against the light. What day was it? As the pounding in my head subsided, a sharp pain coursed through my back. A groan escaped me as my entire body stiffened. The door to my cell swung open and an ocelot in a nurse's outfit walked in, followed by Gideon. I smiled weakly at my long lost brother.

"Hey, Gideon," I muttered, weakly.

His pretty hazel eyes shone as he looked at me. "Scarlet, this is Dotti, she's been cleaning your wounds for these past two days."

My jaw slackened and my eyes widened slightly.

43

"T-two days?" I stammered, then cringed as Dotti lifted the back of my shirt.

Gideon slowly nodded, concern riddling his face. "Yeah...two days."

I retracted from Dotti as she pulled the bandages away from the gashes, her cold paws touching my back as she applied new ones. Gideon lingered in my cell after the ocelot had left. Sitting by my side, he shared a secret smile with me.

"I have good news."

My ears straightened. "Really? What?"

"Your friends are here. Jayden and Sasha, also."

A grin broke out across my face, my eyes brightened. "Really? Gideon, that's great news!" I exclaimed, furrowing my brow. "What about Amos?"

The light brown fox slapped his forehead. "I can't believe I forgot my own twin!"

Chuckling, I shook my head. "Well, at least I know he's here. Okay, do you know where Enigma is? Wait, do you even know who Enigma is?"

My brother nodded. "Yeah, I know where and who he is."

With a sigh of relief, I took him by the shoulders. "Okay, I need you to tell him I'm fine. Ask him if he has a plan."

The hazel eyes specked with green gazed at me, puzzled. "A plan for...?"

I ran a paw through his thick fur. "Just ask him if he has a plan. He'll know what I mean."

Gideon gave me a mock salute. "Sir, yes, sir! Right away, sir!"

I tried my best to give him a stern look, but a smile played at the corners of my mouth.

"It's ma'am to you, Gideon!" I called after him as he left the room.

I stiffly laid down, on my stomach, on the bed. So, everyone I knew and trusted were here. I sighed, staring at the wall. *I wonder if Enigma has a plan. He'd better*, I thought to myself when a knock came at the cell door. I sat up quickly, then groaned. I was going to have to remember those wounds.

"Come in," I called, cringing.

Amos stepped into the room and I gasped with delight.

"Amos! Little bro!"

He laughed and closed the door. "Hey, sis! I heard Coal gave you quite a beating."

I cringed again. "Like you wouldn't believe!"

Walking over to the bed, Amos sat beside me. He looked at me with curious hazel eyes. "How did you ever get yourself into this mess?"

"I've been asking myself the same question, Amos. I hear Jayden is here," I replied, chuckling.

Amos looked away, his eyes narrowing.

"Yeah. After all this time, too. He must want something."

I rolled my eyes. "Or maybe he just wants to help."

Amos snickered and glanced at me. "I doubt it."

"Come on, Amos, just because he left doesn't mean he's all bad."

The fur along Amos's spine stood on end. "Maybe it doesn't, but I still don't trust him."

I chuckled again. "I didn't say I did."

The dirty blond fox gave me a lopsided smile, then wrapped an arm around my neck and pulled me close.

"I missed you, Scarlet."

Laughing softly, I closed my eyes. "Same here."

CHAPTER 9

Lucas swaggered into the P.A.W cafeteria followed closely by Amos. The pair made their way over to Cody and Gideon. Looking up, Cody bristled.

"Here comes trouble..." he mumbled to Amos.

Even though he knew Gideon and Amos were twins, he thought that Gideon was a little more reckless than his younger-by-two-minutes twin.

Gideon grinned wolfishly at Amos as he sat across from him. "Hey, little bro!"

Amos smirked and ran a paw through his fur, ruffling it slightly. "Hey, my older yet shorter brother."

They did this to each other often, making comments about each other. Cody looked solemnly at Lucas.

"Did you get what Ivan wanted?"

The Rottweiler looked up at his adversary. "Maybe I did an' maybe I didn't. Why do you care?"

Cody pointed a claw at himself. "Because *I'm* Ivan's new right paw dog. If *you* didn't get it, then I'm in big trouble with that psycho wolverine who calls himself Ivan the Terrible!"

Amos leaned forward onto the table, looking at the Karelian bear dog. "Now, calm down, Cody. Who said we didn't get it? Gem was more than happy to give us the information, right, Lucas?"

The Rottweiler gave Amos a warning glance, but nodded. "Right."

Gideon chuckled and leaned back in his chair. "Well, I'm glad to see everyone is getting along."

Suddenly, a dark grey fox walked into the cafeteria. Her ears twitched at every little sound, flinching at every loud noise. Cody and Lucas looked at her, obviously puzzled and curious.
"Who's that?" Cody asked in a hushed voice.

Gideon and Amos looked at each other knowingly then back at the fox. Sasha had put dye in her fur so that Cody wouldn't recognize her. She walked nervously up to the table and slid into the seat next to Gideon. Sasha knew she had to play the part of the new girl. She just hoped she could.

"Gideon, aren't you going to introduce me to your

friends?" she asked, looking at Cody and Lucas.

She squinted one eye and let one ear flatten. Amos stifled a laugh and looked away. Gideon smiled sweetly at her.

"Of course! That big brute on the other side of the table is Lucas and this scrawny twig of a dog is Cody."

Cody and Lucas bristled. "Brute?!" said one, while the other said, "Twig of a dog!"

Gideon chuckled. "Guys, this is NightWish. NightWish, meet Cody and Lucas."

Sasha nodded her head in small jerky movements, her other ear flattening as well.

"Nice to meet you."

Cody and Lucas glanced at each other, Lucas raised an eyebrow.

"Okay, Gideon...you and your...friend can take watch over that Savine fox. Are we clear?"

Gideon got a very serious look on his face, narrowed his eyes and nodded in a determined way.

"Crystal clear!"

Standing, he took Sasha by the arm and basically dragged her out of the cafeteria.

Sasha looked at Gideon with wide eyes. "Gideon, now's our cha-" she began, only to be cut off by a paw over her mouth.

Gideon glared at her severely. "Be quiet, Sasha! It's not time yet! We can't rescue you-know-who until Enigma comes up with a plan, got it?"

Sasha slowly nodded her head.

"Good. Now, when I move my paw away from your mouth, don't talk in such a loud voice!"

The light brown paw moved slowly way from her snout. Sasha let out a sigh and sucked in air.

"You were nearly suffocating me, Gideon!"

He rolled his eyes. "Oh, well, forgive me, your highness. Come on, let's go guard Scarlet."

The pair walked down the hallway, their claws clicking against the floor. A security camera zoomed in on them. The little red light blinked, signaling that it was filming. In the control room, Ivan's lips curved into a chilling smile.

"So, my old pal Enigma is back..." he licked his lips and chuckled contently. "Well, let's not keep him waiting. Guards, search the entire building, top to bottom. Leave no door unopened."

The security Rottweilers and Dobermans dispersed out the door, taking different routes into P.A.W. headquarters. Ivan chuckled again and watched the red fox sitting in the prison cell. His brown eyes flickering as the light from the screen bounced off of them, he laughed coldly.

"It's time to bring these so called heroes down to my level."

CHAPTER 10

Enigma sat beside Jayden on the ledge of the building overlooking the valley. Jayden glanced at him, then looked back at the old dirt road that led to freedom. The grey wolf cast a sidelong glance at him.

"We'll get Scarlet out of here. You know that, right?"

Jayden barely moved his eyes to look at Enigma. "I know that, but that's not what I'm thinking."

"Then, what, oh brilliant-minded fox, are you thinking?" Enigma said, rolling his eyes.

Frosty blue eyes stared hard at the wolf. "I'm thinking of a plan, like *you* should be."

Enigma chuckled and stretched his neck. "Look, pup, I already have one in mind. I'm just waiting for the right moment to put it into play."

Jayden shook his head and tensed. "I should be the

one in there instead of Sasha. I'm the smarter one out of both Scarlet and Sasha."

Enigma turned his head to look at the black fox. "Listen, foxy, I don't care what you say, but I *know* you're not smarter than Scarlet. She probably already has put some plan of hers into action. Got it? I don't know how you know the Savine's, but it's obvious you don't know them very well."

The black lips curled back into a sneer. "Apparently, Scarlet hasn't told you much. She probably doesn't even *trust* you! You don't know who I am or why I even care about her, *which* shows you how much she trusts you!"

Enigma immediately bristled and curled a paw into a fist. "Why, you cheeky lit-"

The door that led to the stairwell slammed open and a dozen Doberman's flooded onto the top of the building, guns raised.

"Hold up your paws and stay where you are!"

Enigma shot a hate-ridden glance at Jayden as he and everyone else raised their paws quickly. A Doberman for each animal walked up and forced their paws behind their backs, handcuffing them. Jayden and Enigma kept casting suspicious looks at each other as the Dobermans led them down the stairwell towards the prison cells. With an ear splitting screech, the door to Enigma's cell opened on rusty hinges. Being thrust forward, Enigma slid on the tile floor until he came to a stop when his leg hit the side of the bed, almost flipping him over onto it. He turned around and groaned in despair. Jayden was also thrust into the cell. The frosty eyes glared at Enigma as he stalked around the edge of the cell. The grey wolf sat lazily on the bed, whose mattress was barely an inch thick, watching Jayden. A guard walked into view as he opened the cell door. Ivan also came into view as he held his gaze on Enigma.

"Hello...Enigma. Long time, no see, da?" Ivan said contemptuously.

Enigma's fur stood on end as he looked at the wolverine. "Maybe, but once in a lifetime is enough for me, Ivan."

The wolverine chuckled, shaking his fur. "Oh, you're not glad to see me?"

"I wouldn't call it glad or happy, gleeful or joyful...more like tremendously terrifying and not needed."

Ivan flashed his incisors at Enigma as he smiled. "You still don't remember me, da?"

Jayden glanced quickly at Enigma, curious. "What does he mean?"

Ivan smirked and his ears flattened against his head. "Me and Enigma go way back. Obviously, he doesn't remember anything at all."

Jayden looked at Enigma again, narrowing his eyes. "Does Scarlet know about this?"

Enigma bristled, the fur along his spine standing on end, lips curling into a snarl. "Of course she does!" looking at Ivan, he continued, "She was there when he first brought it up. I don't remember you at all, Ivan! No way, no how!"

Ivan looked contemptuously at them, a small smile creeping up his snout.

"Keep these two in their cell. No food or water, for three days."

Back around the corner Ivan disappeared along with the guard. Jayden watched Enigma with a deep curiosity, his blue eyes tracking every movement the grey wolf made. With a deep sigh, Enigma plopped down onto the bed and put his head in his paws, his ears laid flat against his head, tail limp by his side and almost touching the floor. Jayden raised an eyebrow and, leaning against the wall, slid down it and sat on the floor, crossing his legs Indian style. With a listening ear, Jayden closed his eyes and paid attention to everything. Every creak, every sigh, every falling pawstep, Jayden heard. Opening one eye, he looked at Enigma with irritation. If this wolf wasn't going to do anything, he was. In fact, Jayden already had a plan forming in his brilliant mind. The true inner sly fox was just beginning to come out to play. With a small, lopsided smile, Jayden went to work in his mind, playing out his plan.

CHAPTER 11

I groaned in agony as Dotti replaced the bandages again. I looked at the little digital clock on the wall, watched the minutes tick by. It was three-thirty! I groaned again, not in agony, but in despair. It had been two days since the last time Gideon and Amos had visited me. Amos hadn't even told me if Enigma had a plan! The ocelot left the small cell, leaving me to figure out a plan. If no one else was, I might as well. I ran a paw through my fur, sighing. *Where to begin...how do I escape this cell?* The security camera just outside my cell slowly turned and pointed at me. I glared at it. I would have to cut the wire on that evil little thing. With what, though? I looked at my claws. These would have to do and they just might be able to pick the lock. Standing up, I made my way casually over to the cell door. After waiting for the camera to turn back around, I quickly clipped the thin red wire, then started on picking the lock. Finally, after what seemed like forever, I heard the satisfying *click* of the lock. Opening the door, I ran down the creepy hallway and, hopefully, to freedom. Rounding the corner, I basically ran into Cody. The Karelian bear dog smiled contemptuously down at me as I took a pace back.

"And where do you think you're going?" he asked, blocking my escape.

My hackles rose as I stared up at him. "I...uh...er...well...I...oh, forget this!"

Clinching my paw tightly, I landed a solid punch on Cody's black jaw, enough to make him stumble backwards, but not enough to knock him out. Sending a swift kick to his stomach, he gasped for air, then straightened and punched my ribs, making me groan in pain. With a hard right punch, Cody caught me by the jaw, then grabbed me by the scruff of my neck, holding me tightly. I glared at him, trying to pry myself loose from his grasp.

Chuckling, Cody shook me roughly. "So, did you really think that weak fight you put up would *really* make a difference?"

Smirking, I cocked my head and narrowed my eyes.

"No, not really. But, maybe this will."

He frowned. "Wha-"

Amos hit him hard over the head with a clay vase, making Cody fall to the ground and release me from his grip. Stepping over him, I winked at Amos.

"Thanks, little bro. Now, let's go get Jayden and Enigma."

The dirty blond fox shook his head. "No, you go get them, I have to go rescue Gideon and Sasha from the evil clutches of Lucas."

I chuckled and patted him on the back. "All right. Try to get outside as fast as you can, got it?"

Nodding, he took off down the hall. Shaking my head, I rolled my eyes. That fox! He always showed up at the right times. How did he do that? I frowned suddenly. Where was Enigma? Where was Jayden? I slapped my forehead. Great. Just great. I didn't even know where to look for them. Groaning, I started down the hallway. Well, one way or another, I was going to come across them.

∞

In the prison cell, Enigma looked over at Jayden. The black fox was slumped forward, head basically in his lap, breathing deeply. Enigma snorted.

"Inconsiderate young pup! Probably doesn't even know the first thing about Scarlet or Sasha. Mister Know-It-All! Cheeky little fellow. Should've been named Cheek!"

Jayden's head bobbed slightly as he began snickering. "Cheek? You should've been named Ugly!"

Enigma snorted and began laughing. "Ugly? Hah! You, Mr. Jayden, are looking at a handsome wolf, more handsome than you!"

The frosty eyes narrowed slightly. "You, handsome? You with your thin fur and brown eyes? Hah, don't make me laugh!"

Swinging his legs over the side of the bed, Enigma sat up and leaned forward. "Oh, so, you think you're handsome? With your creepy blue eyes that are almost transparent? Wow, I bet your kind has a low standard for looks! For your information, my eyes are blue!"

Jayden wrinkled his snout and snorted. "What would *you* know about looks? I can see why Scarlet doesn't trust you!"

Paws clinched tightly, Enigma stood stiffly. "Who said Scarlet doesn't trust me?"

Sneering at him, Jayden rolled his eyes and snorted again. "Well, if she did, you would know more about her!"

Frustrated and shaking with anger, Enigma took a step towards the lounging fox. "I do know about her!"

In one swift move, Jayden was suddenly standing. He cocked his head. "For example...?"

Enigma smirked in a victorious manner. "For example she told me how she lost her mother!"

Eyes widening ever so slightly, Jayden stared in Enigma in disbelief. "She did?"

Crossing his arms, Enigma gave a sharp nod. "Yeah, she did."

Jayden frowned and licked his lips in an uncertain way. "How did she?"

"She thinks in a car accident."

A smile crept up Jayden's face, which turned into a grin. He started laughing as he shook his black head.

"Oh, Enigma, I feel for you, dog!"

Enigma frowned in confusion. "What do you mean?"

Catching his breath, Jayden smirked at Enigma. "Her mother didn't die in a car accident and I see she never told you about her father."

"What do you mean, she didn't die in a car accident? Scarlet wouldn't lie to me!"

Jayden snorted again and raised an eyebrow. "Why? Because she trusts you? If she did, she would've told you that her parents died in a house fire and she thought she had lost a brother as well!"

Enigma quickly avoided Jayden's gaze, turning his back on him. "Why didn't she tell me?"

A cruel snicker escaped Jayden. "Maybe for the same reason you haven't told her about yourself, am I right, Kyle?"

Clinching a paw, Enigma slowly turned around to face the black fox. "Or, maybe she doesn't want to get hurt. Ever think of that?"

Jayden sneered at him again. "What're you going to do, kill me? Oh, I'm *so* scared!"

With two quick steps towards the black fox, Enigma planted a hard right punch on Jayden's jaw, making the fox spin around. Grabbing Jayden by the scruff of his neck, Enigma sank his teeth into Jayden's left shoulder. With a high pitched yelp, Jayden turned on his attacker and punched him in the stomach, then another punch landed on Enigma's nose. Releasing Jayden's shoulder, Enigma gasped for air, falling to one knee. Gnashing his teeth, Jayden circled Enigma, his hackles raised, breathing hard.

"You should've stayed away from Scarlet! She'll never trust anyone! You should know that by now. I mean," he curled his lips into a sneer, "she hasn't even told you about the rest of her family."

Anger reared its twisted face inside Enigma. He lifted his head and glared at Jayden. "Shut up!"

Putting a paw on his shoulder, Jayden winced. Blood was pouring from the wound Enigma had inflicted upon him. Laughing harshly, the frosty eyes pierced through Enigma.

"You know I'm telling the truth. Look at the facts, Kyle! She *lied* to you," he dragged the word *lied* out through clinched teeth, smirking. "Scarlet lied to you about how her parents died. Does that penetrate through your thick skull? She *lied* to you!"

Enigma got his footpaw back under him. He stood back up, lips edging back. Stretching his neck, Enigma flexed his paws as Jayden continued his rant.

"Scarlet doesn't trust anyone, Kyle! No one! Not even me! Not even her own siblings! What does that tell you?! Scarlet never trusted you, no matter what she's told you, it was all a *lie*!"

A wild yell ripped out of Enigma's throat as he hurled himself at the black fox. Catching the fox in the midriff, the air was forced out of Jayden's lungs, as the pair flew through the air. Hitting the ground with a crash, the back of Jayden's head connected with the tile floor, a moan escaped him, then he lay still. Shaking with rage, Enigma grabbed the fox by his shirt collar with one paw, then the other paw slammed into Jayden's jaw. Throwing his paw back, Enigma was about to claw Jayden across the face, when he heard claws clicking against the floor. Fearing that it was a prison guard, Enigma picked up the limp form of Jayden and threw him into the bed, as if he was asleep.

∞

That's when I rounded the corner.

"Enigma!" I exclaimed, when I saw his face was beaten and battered with blood running down from his nose.

Instantly smiling, Enigma grasped the bars of the cell. "Savine! How'd you get out?"

Rolling my eyes, I tapped my forehead with a claw. "My ingenious mind figured out a plan when you and your posse didn't show up."

Getting a sheepish smile, Enigma's ears flattened against his head. "Yeah, sorry about that, but as you can see, I was a little caught up. Come on, Savine, get me out of here!"

Picking the lock, I opened the door to the cell. "Where's Jayden?"

Enigma frowned and cocked his head. "Jayden? Who's Jayden?"

Narrowing my eyes, I crossed my arms. "Come on, Enigma, we haven't got all day, *where* is he?!"

Another moan escaped Jayden as he swung his legs over the side of the bed.

"Here I am..." he said, weakly, wincing when he accidently put pressure on his injured shoulder.

Gasping, I ran over to him. "Jayden! What happened to you?!" I froze, then turned on one footpaw and glared at Enigma. "Did you two have a fight?!"

Stiffening, Enigma narrowed his eyes. "Yeah, we did. So, what?"

Clinching a paw, I let out a frustrated groan, then turned and started helping Jayden stand.

"Woah, woah! Just leave him, he doesn't matter!" Enigma blurted out, grabbing me by my arm.

Ripping out of his grasp, I whirled on him, raising a paw. "Didn't I tell you once not to touch me?!"

Glaring at Jayden, he sighed. "Fine, sorry! Just leave him! He'll only slow us down!"

The black fox snorted. "Slow y'all down?! I was only injured on the shoulder!"

Blocking Enigma's view of Jayden, I glared back at him. "Besides, I won't leave him!"

Flattening his ears, the wolf bristled. "Why not?!"

"He's my brother, that's why!"

Enigma's jaw slackened, eyes widening, he looked past me at Jayden.

"*That* cheeky young pup, is your *brother*?!"

Chuckling, I nodded. "Yes, that cheeky young pup is my brother and he's two years *older* than me."

Getting a defiant look on his face, Enigma turned away from me. "Then, grab him and let's go!"

Smiling triumphantly, I pulled Jayden up so he was standing. Looking down at me, Jayden ran a paw through my fur and ruffled it.

"Come on, sis, let's hurry up. I don't want to be caught by any of those guards!"

As we both quietly laughed, we picked up our pace as Enigma picked up his.

CHAPTER 12

Amos ran straight into Lucas, the thick dog looked down at him and raised an eyebrow.

"And just where do you think you're going?" he asked, cocking his head.

"Er...er...I'm just going to go see my brother and his friend."

Narrowing his eyes, Lucas peered closely at the dirty blond fox. "That's the *only* place you're going?"

Giving an affirmative nod, Amos stared right back into the black eyes of Lucas.

"Yes, sir. That is the only place I am going."

A small smile played at the corners of Lucas' mouth. "Good. Off you go then!"

Walking stiffly past Lucas, Amos waited till he was certain no one was watching him, then he sped down the hall, claws clicking repeatedly against the floor.

Reaching the torture chamber, Amos quickly opened the door. Gideon and Sasha were chained against the wall, paws held high above their heads in metal shackles. Their heads hanging limply down, the only visible sign that they were alive was that their chests rose and fell with their shallow breathing. Hurriedly getting the keys to the shackles, Amos speedily undid the shackles holding Gideon. The older twin fox collapsed to the floor with a heavy sigh and a thud. Kneeling down beside him, Amos rolled the brown fox over onto his back.

"Gideon! Gideon, can you hear me? Answer me, for crying out loud!"

Gideon didn't move or answer him, just lay there, mouth slightly agape and his entire body limp. Amos shook Gideon with all his might.

"Gideon, answer me! Please!" he cried out, looking down at his brother.

Suddenly, just when Amos was about to lose hope, a moan escaped from the brown fox. With a shiver of joy, Amos shook his brother again, gentler this time.

"Gideon! Gideon, answer me! Say something!"

The brown eyelids fluttered open, the hazel eyes flecked with green looked up at Amos in agony, the bottom jaw moved, but only a murmur of words slipped out. Leaning down, his ear pressed close to Gideon's snout, Amos frowned.

"What did you say?"

"I said, get off my tail!" yelled Gideon, finally recovering his voice.

Leaping backwards, Amos put a paw to his ear.

"Okay, okay! You didn't have to yell!"

Propping himself up on his elbows, Gideon rolled his eyes. "Well, what's the point in telling you you're on my tail if I can't yell?"

Sasha's tail moved slightly, then she lifted her head with great effort. Smiling weakly, the grey fox looked at her brothers.

"Okay, I'm glad that we're having a great family reunion and I'd hate to be the one to be such a burden, but...could y'all take a second and get me out of these shackles?! They're starting to hurt my wrists!" she whined piteously.

Amos instantly went to work at opening the metal shackles binding her to the wall.

"Oh, yes, your majesty! Anything for you!" Amos replied sarcastically, putting on a terrible British accent.

With a final click, the last shackle fell from Sasha's

wrists. Rubbing the raw spots on her wrists, she looked at the twins.

"All right, let's go find the others and get *out* of here!" she said, starting to walk to the door, when two luminous figures seemed to materialize out of nowhere.

Stepping down into the torture chamber, Cody grinned mockingly at the trio.

"I don't think that's going to be as easy as it sounds," he said, letting his eyes look over the trio.

Coal stood beside him, licking his lips eagerly.

"Now can I, boss?" he said, his tail swaying side to side, as he looked at his new prisoner. Amos.

Cody pointed a black claw at Sasha. "Bring her to me, Coal."

Getting a disappointed look on his face, the black wolf slunk up to the grey fox, towering over her. Seizing her roughly by the arm, he thrust Sasha at Cody. His ears laying flat against his head, Cody looked down at Sasha, a playful smile on his face.

"Long time no see, right, Sasha?"

Standing her ground, Sasha planted her footpaws firmly on the tile. "I could do another ten years without seeing you again, Cody," she said, looking up at him, a deep growl coming from her chest. "When was the last time I saw you...oh, yeah, you had betrayed us! You had been paid off by those dogs! You betrayed my sister! You betrayed *me*! How could you?!"

Cody grabbed Sasha's arm and pushed her, not too gently, out the door.

"Coal, do what you will to those two," he said over his shoulder, then slammed the door shut. Glaring at Sasha, he kept pushing her forwards, forcing her to walk.

A deep growl emitted from deep in Sasha's chest. "Where are you taking me, Cody?"

The chilling laugh sent a cold shiver down Sasha's spine. "You're going to meet a friend of mine. I'm pretty sure y'all have met."

The duo arrived at a pair of double doors. Sasha looked up at her captor.

"What? Am I supposed to be scared of these doors?"

A sneer formed on Cody's black and white face. "You should be!"

Opening one of the doors, Cody shoved Sasha into Ivan's office. Taking a sharp breath in, Sasha stared at the magnificent wolverine. A warm smile crossed the wolverine's face when he saw the grey fox.

"Oh, hello, there! You are Scarlet's sister, da?" he

asked, clasping his paws together and resting his elbows on the desk.

Nodding in jerky movements, Sasha felt her fears rising up inside her.

The mocking laugh shook Sasha to her core. "You're afraid of me, da?"

Swallowing hard, Sasha forced herself to keep a poker face. "No!"

Lips curling back over his teeth, Ivan snarled. "You should be! I can rip you to shreds! I can make your life vanish!"

Paws shaking, Sasha swallowed again. "I'm not afraid of you!" she stated, trying to keep her voice steady as she locked eyes with Ivan.

Smirking, Ivan slowly stood up from his chair and, walking around the desk, made his way to Sasha. Keeping his distance from her, he walked in a circle around her.

"It was a sad day," he said, his voice barely a whisper.

Cocking her head, Sasha frowned. "What do you mean?"

"I mean, it was a sad day both your parents died," he said in a taunting tone. "It was a house fire, no?"

Shaking his head, a mocking sigh escaped his lips. "The police never did find out how it started. No?"

Bristling, Sasha looked directly at Ivan. "And what would you know about it?"

Ivan shrugged lazily, a sly smile creeping up his snout. "More than you do, I'll bet."

Snorting, Sasha shook her head. "I doubt that."

Leaning on a chair, Ivan stretched his legs out. "Want to bet on that?"

Looking over at him, she narrowed her eyes and rolled them. "Fine. But, no matter what you say, I know it'll be wrong."

"Oh, like, me knowing that your father worked with P.U.G.?"

Freezing, Sasha glanced at him. "How did you know that?"

"I know everything. Nothing escapes my knowledge."

Again, Sasha snorted. "I seriously doubt that."

"I know how that fire was started."

Sasha didn't move.

"If you want to know how, you're going to have to do something for me."

Avoiding his gaze, Sasha muttered, "What do you

want me to do?"

Having her just where he wanted her, Ivan knew this was his only chance to defeat the only animal that could ruin everything.

"Bring Scarlet to me."

Quickly looking up, Sasha hesitated. "Is that all?"

Grinning triumphantly, Ivan nodded. "That's all."

"First, tell me what you know."

Raising an eyebrow, Ivan tilted his head slightly. "How do I know you won't betray me?"

Sasha smiled weakly. "You're the one that said you can tear me to shreds."

A small smile played on Ivan's snout. "True, da?" Ivan paused for a second, and then looked up at Sasha. "I had the fire started. Every beast was in the house. You, Scarlet, those reckless twins and Jayden, and your parents. Coal put a match on the curtains. Soon, the fire was licking the ceiling, and then Coal fled the building. Your father, as I have said, was working for P.U.G. So was your mother. In fact, your father helped the guy who started P.U.G. once he learned about my plans. I had to do something, no?"

Tears brimmed along Sasha's eyelids. One slipped down her face and fell to the floor with a splash. Paws shaking with rage, she blinked back the tears and sniffed. Ears flattening against her head, she finally looked up at the wolverine. Her body shook with a sob, Sasha clinched her paws tightly together.

"So...you're the one who had my parents killed?" she asked through gritted teeth.

A huge grin appeared on Ivan's face. "Da. I couldn't let them ruin my plans, now, could I?"

Lips curling back over her teeth, Sasha snarled at him. "*You* killed them!"

"Da, I just agreed with you," he said, frowning.

Leaping at the wolverine, a bloodcurdling yell emitted from Sasha's throat as she sank her teeth into Ivan's shoulder. Growling in pain, Ivan grabbed Sasha around the spine, sinking his claws deep into her flesh. Yelping, Sasha instantly let go of Ivan. Flinging the fox across the room, Ivan snarled at his foe. Hitting the wall with a sickening thud, Sasha fell to the floor. Stalking over to her, Ivan picked her up by the scruff of her neck, bringing her close to his snout. Sasha grimaced when she smelt his foul breath.

"You really need a breath mint," she muttered with a weak smile.

Cody had been standing in the doorway the entire

time, now he closed the doors, for he knew what Ivan was going to do next. An agonizing, painful, bloodcurdling scream echoed down the empty halls of P.A.W. headquarters. Cody cringed and looked back at the double doors as he kept walking.

"There died Sasha Savine, sister of the one and only Scarlet Savine," he muttered, then disappeared down the hall.

CHAPTER 13

I bet everyone in P.A.W. headquarters heard that chilling scream. We stopped dead in our tracks. Feeling the hackles rise along my spine, I looked over at Jayden and Enigma.

"What in the world was *that*?" I asked, shaking the eerie feeling from myself.

Enigma looked up and down the halls, watching for guards. "I have no idea, but I don't like it. Let's keep moving."

As Enigma rounded the corner, he ran straight into Cody. The Karelian bear dog froze, looking from me to Enigma as if afraid. The wolf instantly grabbed Cody by the collar of his shirt.

"Where do you think you're going?" he growled, pulling Cody snout to snout.

Gulping, Cody shook his head. "N-n-nowhere!"

I peered over Enigma's shoulder so I could look at Cody. "You've never stuttered before. Why now?"

Cody avoided looking at me. "M-me? Stutter? Hah! I-I'm not st-st-stuttering!"

"Yes, you are!" Jayden informed him, laughing coldly.

Suddenly, Cody grinned. "Guards! Guards! Over here!"

Whirling around, Jayden and I stood facing at least a dozen Doberman guards. Turning around, Enigma held a knife to Cody's throat.

"One step closer and I'll slice his throat!" he called out, looking wildly from one guard to the next.

"I don't think you will," came a familiar chilling voice.

Slowly, we turned back around. Ivan stood towering over us like some monstrous nightmare. Blood dripping from his snout, a wound on his shoulder, he looked down at us. His eyes fixed on me, his lips curling about.

"One sister remains, da?"

Frowning, I glared curiously up at him. "What do you mean?"

"Where do you think this blood came from?" he

said, smirking. "Your sister was a poor fighter."

I stopped breathing as fear raised its ugly head, then I snarled, "Where is she, Ivan?!"

Glancing down the hallway at his office, Ivan smiled chillingly. "I don't think you'll find much there."

Running as I have never run before, I reached the doorway of Ivan's office. A limp form lay on its side in a pool of crimson blood on the floor. I held my breath as I neared the body. With a trembling paw, I reached out towards Sasha.

Grabbing her shoulder gently, I rolled her over. Claw marks gouged deep in her face, I could barely tell that she was my sister. Suddenly, she started to cough and spit up frothy red blood.

"Scarlet," she gasped out between sickening, gurgling coughs, "I know what happened to our...parents!"

Shaking uncontrollably, I kneeled beside her. "Sh, be quiet, Sasha. Don't try to talk, you'll choke on your own blood!"

Grabbing my paw in hers, she coughed harder, blood dribbling down from her gaping mouth, down her cheek and running along her neck. "Ivan had Coal set fire to the house, Scarlet! J-justice m-must be s-served!"

With a deep gurgle that came from her throat, she lay limply on the floor and her amber eyes glazed over. Caught short of breath, I fell onto my knees as I stared at Sasha. A broken sob shook my entire body, tears poured down my face and splashed on the floor. With shaking paws, I covered my face, crying hard. Jayden ran in, saw the limp form on the floor and froze. A deep breath escaped his lips as he, almost as if in a trance, walked into the room. Kneeling beside me, he pulled me close to him, keeping me from looking at Sasha. Through sobs, I tried to speak.

"What kind of monster could do this?" I choked out, to no one in particular.

Jayden didn't reply or move, just held me close to himself. Pulling away from my brother, I looked back at the mangled body of Sasha. Blood dripped from the gashes on her face, gouges across her throat and her shredded ear. A broken sob escaped me, shaking my entire body. How could this have happened? Why her?

"Why her? Why? It should've been me! Never her! No!" I cried out, my face raised skywards.

Paws grabbed me by my shoulders and hoisted me up to where I was standing, then the animal spun me around. I gazed into the deep blue eyes of Enigma.

"Scarlet! Stop talking like that! If it had been you, no one would've been able to continue on! No one! Not even Sasha!" he cried, looking earnestly into my eyes.

Another sob escaped me as I shook my head dumbly, tears clouding my vision. "I should've been the one killed!"

Jayden sprung up from his sitting position. "Shut up, Scarlet! Stop talking like that! You know it was her time! If it hadn't been now, it might have been worse!"

Eyes ablaze, I glared at him. "*How* could it have been worse, Jayden?!"

"It could've been a long drawn out death, like cancer!"

I clamped my jaw shut.

Enigma looked at me, eyes serious. "There's one thing left to do, Scarlet."

Furrowing my brow, I looked out the window when I heard the sound of a helicopter. The helicopter slowly lifted into the air, the letters P.A.W. printed in large white lettering on the side. Then, I knew what I had to do.

CHAPTER 14

Ivan looked over at his three most trusted companions. Lucas O'Meara, Gem Firewater and Cody Haner. The Karelian bear dog looked over the side of the helicopter and swallowed hard.

"Did I ever mention I'm afraid of heights?" he asked, nervously.

Gem's black tail seemed to have a life of its own as it swished back and forth, she softly laughed.

"It figures a dog would be afraid of heights, never having been on the tiniest branch of the tree high up in the sky as the wind blows relentlessly, every move you make could be your last," she said, smoothing her tail out.

Lucas chuckled as he looked at the black cat. "Well, I'm not afraid, Gem. How do you explain that?"

Getting an irritated look, Gem gave him a mocking

smile. "Easy! You've been in and out of helicopters your entire life. You're use to them."

Ivan tapped his claws on the arm rest in a steady rhythm, thinking deeply and urgently.

"I have a feeling that Scarlet and her friends will not easily give up as y'all said they would," he said in a low monotone.

Tail flicking back and forth irately, Gem raised an eyebrow. "Do you think we have lied to you? I know Scarlet. The death of her sister will affect her greatly. The two were very close. It will cause her much grief."

Ivan narrowed his eyes and looked out the window, pondering Gem's words.

"Or," he began slowly, "It will have the complete opposite effect on her. The death of Sasha may urge her to continue her quest and try to defeat my organization. Sasha's death may just have been the thing Scarlet needed to fuel her urgency. I think I made a grave mistake in killing that grey fox."

Lucas gave a reassuring look at Ivan. "You knew what you were doing, you made the right choice. Trust me!"

Nodding, both Gem and Cody smiled at Ivan. "Trust us, Ivan! We know Scarlet! She won't do anything now that Sasha is dead!"

Raising an eyebrow, Ivan looked at his companions. "Y'all had better hope you're right. If *not*," he flexed his paw, long black curved claws shining in the gleam of the sunlight, "You know what I can do, da?"

Quickly nodding, the trio smiled nervously. "Yes, boss! We know what you can do!"

Smiling wickedly, Ivan looked out the window again. "Good. If Scarlet and her companions do decide to come for me, y'all will be the first ones to know," he said, eyes narrowing to thin slits as he watched the towns and cities pass by under the helicopter.

CHAPTER 15

Coal laughed mercilessly as he hit Amos on the back with the leather whip. The dirty blond fox cringed, but kept the scream of agony inside. Gideon had been chained back to the wall, awaiting his turn to be beaten. Spying the keys on a table not too far from him, Gideon began to form a plan in his mind. Somehow get the keys, break out of these shackles, take Coal down and rescue his brother. Yeah, that seemed like a good plan. How was he going to get the keys? Groaning, Gideon stomped his footpaw against the tile floor. A light bulb went off in his head. His footpaws weren't shackled! Taking a deep breath, Gideon stuck a footpaw out towards the table, reaching for the keys with his toes. Just a few more inches and he would have them! Stretching with all his might, his toes came just short of being able to grab the keys. In one last, desperate attempt to grab them, he kicked out with his footpaw. As if in slow motion, the keys flew off the table, up into the air and landed on the tile floor with a clink. Coal stopped what he was doing, which was beating Amos, to turn around to try and find the source of the sound. Making eye contact with Gideon, Coal walked over to the light brown fox.

"What was that sound?" he asked, tilting his head.

Shrugging lazily, Gideon looked casually around the room. "I don't know. Maybe a torturing instrument of yours?"

Amos saw his chance. Twisting his paws, he began tugging at the ropes constraining him. With a grunt, Amos pulled one paw free. Not hearing Amos, Coal looked down and saw the keys on the floor.

"What is this?" he said, bending down and picking them up. Looking suspiciously at Gideon, he shook the keys in front of the fox's nose. "Trying to escape, are you?"

Bristling, Gideon struck out with his footpaw, catching the black wolf in the ribs. Caught by surprise, Coal stumbled backward from the force of the blow and right into Amos's southpaw. Hitting the ground with a hollow thud, Coal looked up into hazel eyes flecked with green. Smiling, Amos went over to Gideon and unshackled him.

"Thanks, bro, couldn't have done it without you!" he said, laughing.

Running a paw through his fur, Gideon rolled his eyes. "Next time, I'll be the one to rescue *you*, got it, little bro?"

Amos laughed again. "Whatever!"

Leaping up to his footpaws, Coal started running out of the room only to be tackled by Gideon. Taken down to the ground, Gideon swung a hard right paw into Coal's jaw. A moan escaped the black wolf, then he was out like a light. Amos smirked.

"Just a *tad* excessive, don't you think, bro?"

"Oh, quit, you would've done the same thing and you know it!"

Laughing, Amos crossed his arms. "Oh, well, if I was going to do it, then...why didn't I?"

"Because I beat you to it!"

"No, you didn't!"

"Yes, I did!"

"Didn't!"

"Did!"

Rounding the corner, I eyed the pair.

"Guys, quit bickering and listen!"

Gideon and Amos instantly looked over at me. "Oh, hey, sis!"

Jayden came up beside me, bearing the limp form of Sasha, which was covered in a loose blanket. Jayden stared fixedly at Gideon. *Finally, after all these years, I can see them both, together…in the same room.* Jayden thought. *The greetings will have to wait though…* The twins froze in horror at the sight of a limp and bloody grey arm dangling down from underneath the blanket. Walking uneasily forward, Amos reached out a paw towards our sister. Taking the blanket in his paw, he pulled it away from her. The gouged face was turned limply to its side, facing him. The lifeless eyes staring back at him, the sagging jaw, the drying blood splattered across her face and down her neck. Gasping in shock, Amos stumbled backwards and collided with the wall. Gideon stared into her eyes, unable to move. Sliding down the wall, Amos sat on the floor staring dumbly at the ground. Turning to my sister, I covered her back up with the blanket. Hackles raised, I turned back to my brothers.

"We need to finish this war. For her. For the world. This is my promise. I will not stop until that barbaric wolverine is either in jail or dead!" I snarled, clinching my paws.

Looking from Enigma to the twins, Jayden nodded his furry black head.

"Then, we are with you to the end, Scarlet," he said.

Gideon offered a paw to Amos, but the dirty blond fox pushed it away and stood up on his own.

"Let's go get that wolverine!" Amos spat the words out through gritted teeth.

Enigma turned to me. "Before we go rushing into who knows what, we need a plan. If we go rushing in there with all rage and no idea what we're getting into, we're dead ducks!"

I paused, and then slowly nodded my head. "Agreed. Where's Silver?"

"In the getaway car in the woods. I told him to wait out there for us."

Turning around, I started down the hall. "Then, let's get out of here!"

Enigma and Jayden lagged towards the back of the group as they were carrying Sasha. Cautiously walking down the hallways, we headed for an exit. As we rounded a corner, we almost bumped into a group of about ten guards. I wasn't in the mood for being captured, as you can imagine. Crouching down, my paws before me with claws flexing, I snarled dangerously. Amos and Gideon were at my sides, eyes slanted and ears flattened. The guards started to pull their weapons, but they had no chance. The three of us were on them like a pack of wolves, tearing and biting viciously. Like lightning, the ten guards were dead. I turned around to face Jayden and Enigma, my chest heaving up and down with my panting. They stood there before me, eyes wide in astonishment.

"Come on, let's go," I muttered, then turned on a heel and carefully stepped over the dead guards.

In silence, they followed me through the halls of P.A.W. I carefully avoided any other confrontations with guards by letting them pass by us. Surprisingly, none saw us. We rounded a corner and I saw a door with a sign above, on a sign in red letters was the magic word. Exit. Fresh tears started slipping down my face as we ran towards the exit. The only exit. There was nothing between us and freedom. Claws clicking on the tile floor, I hit the door with a slam. Fresh air hit me like a cold slap to the face. Taking in a deep breath, I kept running. With my friends behind me, I knew where to go. The only place Ivan would go. Behind me, a deep mournful howl split across the night sky. I looked over my shoulder to see Enigma, face to the sky, howling. He was answered by a deeper, more powerful howl. Silver! A black SUV came speeding out of the woods, gravel crunching under its tires. Coming to a sudden halt, Silver hopped out of the car.

"What happened to Sasha?" he asked, looking at the limp form.

Enigma shook his head. "I'll tell you on the way, just get in the car! We're going after Ivan for the final time!"

Silver slipped back into the car. "Okay, okay. Come on, then, get in!"

Sliding into the back of the car, I found Will to be sitting beside me. A tear slipped down his face and splashed against the seat.

"I'm going to tear that wolverine to bits," he muttered, in a barely audible tone.

I glared out the window, clinching my paws. "Not if I get to him first."

CHAPTER 16

The helicopter landed on the top of CIA headquarters. Getting out, Ivan was followed by the trio. The blades of the helicopters propeller slowed to a deep *whump whump* as the four animals made their way into the building. No beast who knew anything dared to look up when they saw the brown wolverine. Any new recruit was quickly silenced when they began to ask questions. Everyone knew why Ivan was here. Everyone had a suspicion, but no one dared to speak up. The entire floor fell into a deafening silence as Ivan made his way to the office. Grasping the doorknob, he pushed the door open. Peter casually looked up from his desk and when he saw it was Ivan, he froze.

"What are you doing here?!" he asked in a hushed voice, his eyes flicking from one side of the room to the other, as if searching for an escape.

Seeming to guess the thoughts going through Peter's head, Ivan held up a paw to silence him.

"There's no escape, Talon. You know why I'm here. Give me my passports," Ivan growled, narrowing his eyes and holding his paw out towards the grey wolf.

Swallowing nervously, Peter reached into a drawer on his desk and pulled out a blue passport.

"Here you go, Ivan."

The wolverine took the little booklet between two claws, not raising his eyes to look at Peter, he murmured, "You know what you have to do."

Peter's eyes widened and he shook his head. "No! No! I'm not going to betray her!"

The sharp black claws tapped rhythmically on the desk top. "You know what will happen if you don't."

His paw clasping his throat, Peter slowly nodded. "Y-yes, sir. I know. I'll do whatever you ask of me!"

Ivan smiled in what he imagined was a friendly way. "Good. I'm glad to hear that."

"But, sir, why do I have to be the one to...to..." he didn't finish his sentence.

Ivan's smile faded. "Why do you have to betray Scarlet? I'll tell you why. You work for *me*, not the CIA. Well, not officially for the CIA, but still. Now, you listen to me *or* you'll never live to see another sunrise, yes?"

Avoiding the deathly gaze of the wolverine, Peter nodded his head solemnly. "Yes, sir. Anything you say, sir."

Turning on one footpaw, Ivan waltzed out of the room. "Glad to know you're on my team, Peter. I'll be in my office."

Once outside the ash grey wolf's office, Ivan grabbed Lucas by the collar of his shirt and pulled him snout to snout. Snarling, Ivan looked into the big brown eyes.

"Have him followed, every move he makes I want to know about it! Anyone who talks to him or even glances at him, I want to know about it! That grey wolf is a weak link in the chain. If he breaks, then the entire chain will fall apart! Peter knows who else is working with us, all our major assets. If even *one* of those names gets leaked, we're doomed, do you understand?"

Nodding quickly, Lucas didn't dare stare back into his boss' eyes. "Understood!"

Releasing his hold on Lucas, Ivan smoothed the shirt out and patted the Rottweiler on the back. "Then, go and," he whispered dangerously into Lucas' ear, "If you fail me again, I will find you. You know that, yes?"

Swallowing hard, the Rottweiler smiled nervously. "Yes, I know."

Turning to Gem, Ivan stared into her eyes. "You go with him."

Tail flicking in an annoyed manner, Gem's ears flattened and a short sigh escaped her. "Fine."

Smiling, Lucas winked at her. "Just like old times, eh, Gem?"

"Oh, shut it, Lucas. I'm not going to enjoy this. I hope you know that."

Laughing softly, Lucas shook his head. "The same old Gem. Oh well, let's go watch Peter."

Standing on either side of Peter's door, the odd pair tried not to make small talk.

CHAPTER 17

My lower jaw trembled as I tried to keep back the tears. I wasn't about to fall apart in front of my friends. Blinking to keep the big drops of tears back, I bit my cheek. No one was going to see me cry. No one. A gentle paw rested on my shoulder, drawing my attention away from the window of the car. Emotionless frosty blue eyes stared at me.

"Jayden...what are you looking at?" I asked, raising an eyebrow.

"You, who else?" he whispered, studying my face.

I shuddered. "That's just a little creepy, Jayden."

He stayed quiet for a while, studying me, watching my eyes. "I know you, Scarlet, I know that you two were close. I'm just concerned for you, that's all."

Snorting, I rolled my eyes. "Worried about me? I can take care of myself. I don't need anyone."

The concern in his eyes turned into worry. "I don't believe that. Everyone needs someone, Scarlet. Even the most independent animal. Even me."

Unable to look away from his holding gaze, my gaze turned deadly serious. "Even you? Like who?"

Hesitating, Jayden's gaze wavered.

I smiled slightly. "Jayden, who?"

"It used to be Mom..." he whispered so quietly I could barely make out the words.

Turning his head, the black fox didn't look at me. A tear slipped down my face, but I brushed it away quickly with a swipe of my paw.

"Oh, I see." Pausing, I shook my head. "But, you're not me, brother. I can and have lived most of my life without needing anyone. I'm fine, really."

Raising his eyes back up, Jayden tilted his head and gave me a knowing smile.

"You and me both know that's a lie," he sighed, "But, if you want it this way, I won't bother you about it."

Enigma looked back at me in the rearview mirror. "Why do you think that Ivan would go to the CIA headquarters?"

Forcing myself to look away from Jayden, I gazed

at the grey wolf.

"Call it a hunch. Trust me, he's there."

Frowning, Enigma looked back at the road. "That's a wild hunch, if you ask me, Savine."

"You don't trust me?" I asked, bristling.

"Well, you don't trust me," he replied, coolly.

"Yeah, I don't. I have no reason to trust you!"

The hackles on his spine rose quickly. "I've given you plenty of reasons to trust me, Savine! Want me to name a few?"

"All right, you two, that's enough! Let's not fight. Not after what happened," Jayden interrupted quickly.

The twins sighed with relief. Grip tightening on the steering wheel, Enigma glared back at me in the rearview mirror. Sneering at him, I looked out the window.

"You're right, Jayden. We'll just save it for another time, another place," I muttered through gritted teeth.

Slowly, I began to recognize the place where we were. The road got busier, shopping malls and stores were everywhere. Animals walking around as if there wasn't a thing wrong with the world. A painful look crossed my face. I used to be one of them, not a care in the world. I didn't have to worry about a war. No reason to be afraid for my life. Then, the CIA building came into view. My heart skipped a beat. This may finally be the end of the war. The end of my worry, the end. Pulling into the parking lot, I didn't even wait for Enigma to stop the car. Opening my door quickly, I leapt out of the car. Gideon watched me with fearful, wide eyes.

"Scarlet, wait! You can't go in there alone!"

The car came to a screeching halt as Enigma slammed on the brakes. A car behind him honked, but he didn't pay attention. Jumping out of the car, Enigma didn't even glance at the others as he barked out orders.

"Jayden, Gideon and Amos! Y'all are coming with us. Silver, go back to the house, get Jack and Will! He'll know what to do. Scarlet, don't argue with me right now, I'm not in the mood!"

Brushing past me, my brothers followed Enigma like puppies. Gritting my teeth in irritation, I had no choice but to follow. Walking through the sliding glass doors, we hurried over to Penelope. The little toy dog looked up, a smile on her face, but it quickly disappeared.

"Savine! Malum!" she began, then saw Will and my brothers. "Ferguson? Who are the others?"

A stern look came across my face. "You weren't expecting us back, were you, Penelope?"

"N-no, uh, I mean, yes! Why wouldn't I expect you back, Savine?" she asked quickly, nervously folding some papers.

"How do you know my real name?" I asked, my voice dangerously low.

"Your r-real name?" she laughed nervously, "Did I say Savine? I meant Carter!"

"That makes no difference! How did you know her last name, Penelope?!" Enigma leaned over the desk and growled deeply.

Shaking uncontrollably, the Pomeranian slumped in her chair. "I-I-I..."

Jayden stood next to Enigma and slammed a fist down on the desktop, making the dog jump. "We're wasting time, asking her how she knew Scarlet's name! Is Ivan here?!"

Nodding her head dumbly, Penelope didn't look up. "Y-yes, he's here."

"Where?!" we asked in unison.

"H-h-he has his own office on the top floor! He always has!"

Turning on one footpaw, I sped over to the elevator.

"It's time to finish this war once and for all!"

Realizing where I was going, Enigma spun around to face me. "Scarlet, no! You can't do it alone!"

The elevator door opened and I stepped into it. "Just watch me!"

Amos started running over to the elevator. "Scarlet! Stop! Keep that door open!"

Following Amos, the others ran after him. Enigma had a panicked look on his face.

"Scarlet, don't!"

"You're the one who dragged me into this, *remember*, Enigma?!" I yelled at him as the doors closed in their faces.

Paws shaking, an unsteady breath escaped me. Fear was raising its ugly head again. Shaking myself out, my fur ruffling, I clinched my paws and gritted my teeth. This was it. This was my last chance to ruin Ivan's plans. This was the end. The doors opened and, expecting a horde of Doberman guards, I leapt out into the hallway yelling. Only to find no one was there. Frowning, I looked up and down the empty hall. Where were they? Turning back to the elevator, I used my pocketknife to pry away the silver plating around the little white buttons. Cutting a few wires, I hoped to stall the others.

The sound of claws clicking on the floor drew my attention away from the elevator. Looking around quickly, I opened a door and slipped into the room. Closing my eyes and sighing, I turned around and froze. At least five Dobermans stared back at me.

"Aw, come on!" I groaned, letting my arms fall to my sides.

The tallest of the Dobermans, who had a nasty scar running from the tip of one ear down to the end of his snout, sneered at me.

"Look who it is, boys!" he said, bowing up. "It's that fox, Scarlet Savine!"

The smallest of the five chuckled like a hyena, his wild eyes looking me over. "Oh, this is a treat, ain't it, Revenge?"

Revenge, the one who had spoken first, touched his lips with the tip of his tongue. "You bet, Joker. Get 'er!"

Apparently, Revenge was this gang's leader, because the other four started towards me, slowly. My hackles rose as I took two steps back with every step they took towards me.

"You know what I did to the last Dobermans who tried to get me?" I asked, trying to be brave.

"Let me guess, ya screamed like a lil' gurl when

they grabbed ya?" Joker snickered evilly.

I laughed along with him, then shook my head. "No, I made them pay for it!"

That didn't seem to faze them much. They just laughed and kept coming. Grabbing a vase, I held it up, threatening to throw it.

"One step closer and I'll smash this into your heads!" I yelled dangerously, hoping to scare them.

It seemed to work! A fearful look passed over their faces as they stopped advancing towards me. Getting a cocky smile, I stood straight and took a step towards them. They took a step back.

"Yeah, that's right! Run along you little pups!" I growled deeply, clinching my fists.

It got the opposite effect. They fell to their knees, faces to the floor.

"No, no! Please don't, sir! Please!" they cried.

I frowned. "Sir? I'm not a si-" I stopped and turned around slowly.

Enigma and Jayden started laughing hard.

"Don't worry, sis, we won't say a thing," Amos said reassuringly, elbowing Gideon in the ribs.

"What? Oh, oh, yes! We won't say a thing!" the light brown fox said quickly.

Stiffening, I glared at Enigma and Jayden. "Oh, y'all think that's funny, do you?! If I did that to either of you, y'all wouldn't think it was funny, would you?!"

Jayden got a mock serious look and turned his gaze to Enigma. "You know, she's right! Stop laughing!"

"Okay, okay. I'm sorry, Scarlet. But, it was funny."

Ears flattened against my head, I growled. "I'm sure it was!"

Gideon cleared his throat. "Well, what are we doing standing around here for? Let's go get that wolverine who killed our sister!"

"Well, you don't have to look any further, da?" came the familiar voice of Ivan.

Looking past Jayden and Enigma, I saw Ivan standing in the hallway. Pushing past the two, I stood in the doorway.

"You!" I snarled, pointing a claw at him.

"Me?" he asked innocently, his once white teeth now bloodstained.

"You killed my sister!" I growled, advancing towards him, but was caught by the arm. Looking over my shoulder, I stared into Enigma's eyes. "Let me *go*, Enigma!"

Shaking his head, he didn't answer. With a sharp

tug, I freed myself from his grasp.

"Yes," Ivan replied in a hushed voice, his tone taunting. "I killed your pitiful sister! Sasha put up a *weak* and *useless* fight! When I sunk my claws into her back, she cried for *help*, but none came! When I hurt her, she cried out to God! Did He answer her? No! He did nothing! Then, I sliced her neck with my claws and *that* was the end of your poor, weak sister!"

Tears ran down my cheeks as my heart raced. Clinching my paws, I snarled at him.

"You don't know what you're talking about! God was there! He did answer her, maybe not in the way she or anyone else wanted, but He did what was right! He did what He knew was right, Ivan! Unlike *you*! My sister was stronger than any of us! Stronger than you!" I said, ignoring the tears. "You'll never know what true strength is! You're *weak*, Ivan! You're weaker than a pup!"

Instantly, a huge paw grabbed me around my throat and pulled me off my footpaws. My friends tried to help, but were hemmed in by Dobermans. Trying to pry his claws away from my neck, Ivan pulled me snout to snout, his foul, hot breath slapping me in the face like a poisonous gas. Smiling briefly, I started gasping for air. Ivan glared at me like a wild mustang.

"What's so funny?" he hissed, spit splattering over my face.

"I think someone needs a breath mint," I said with great effort.

With a wild roar like a lion, he hurled me across the room. Hitting the floor, what air was left in my lungs was knocked out of me. Getting a footpaw under me, I started to get up, but was picked up off my footpaws again and slammed into the wall. Snout to snout again, Ivan snarled wickedly and started chuckling, slobber dripping from his mouth.

"What do you say *now*, Scarlet? Do you still think I'm weak?" he said, hissing out the words.

"Y-yes, I still think you're weak!" I said, between gasps of air.

Whirling around, he threw me into the other side of the hall. I hit my back against the wall and fell to the ground, groaning. Leaping through the air like some dark animal, I saw his fangs and claws flash, another wild roar ripped out of his throat. My life flashed before my eyes, heart pounding, I closed my eyes and screamed at the top of my lungs. A whoosh of air swept over me and I knew it was the end of my life. But, no deadly fangs caught my throat! No claws slashed across my face! No hurt, no wound! I reluctantly opened my eyes. A black furry shape was on top of Ivan, biting and scratching. Jayden! Looking back toward Enigma, I found that the others were fighting the Dobermans! A cool wave of relief washed over me like a refreshing drink of water. I wasn't going to die just yet! Just as I was about to relax, a piercing yelp hit me. Looking back to Jayden, I instantly snarled. Ivan had pinned my older brother to the ground. Getting my footpaws under me, I hurled myself at the wolverine. Digging my claws into his shoulders, I grabbed his ear in my teeth and bit down hard, then sharply tugged my head to the side. With a cry of agony, Ivan let go of Jayden and started to try to get me off him. Spitting a piece of fur from my mouth, I sunk my teeth into the side of his neck. Swinging his paws over his head, he grabbed my back and ripped me off him with a swift jerk. Sliding across the floor, I hit the wall again. Jayden crouched down, his muscles tensing, the black fox snarled at the monstrous figure looming over him. A deep growl emitted from deep inside Ivan's chest like a car engine revving. Paw rising high into the air, shiny black claws flickering in the light, Ivan prepared to land the fatal blow to Jayden. The click of the hammer on a pistol stopped the wolverine.

CHAPTER 18

"Turn around, Ivan, slowly," Enigma's voice rang out.

A sneer crossed Ivan's bloody face as he turned around. "So, you're going to kill me, da?"

"There would be no greater pleasure, believe me! But, I believe the killing belongs to someone else. Someone like Scarlet or one of her brothers."

Ivan started laughing, a hollow laugh. Scary and icy. "I knew you couldn't kill me! You're weak! Just like your father!"

I watched Enigma's face go from full of life to stiff and emotionless. "What do you mean? My father was the strongest of any of the leaders of P.U.G.!"

Ivan licked his lips contently. "He cowed like the

weak wolf he was when we got into the fatal fight!"
Sneering, Ivan shrugged carelessly. "Fatal for one, at
least. Your father didn't stand a chance!"

Enigma now held the pistol with two paws, his
breathing more rapid. "Stop talking! You don't know
what you're saying!"

Ivan held his paws out in a submissive manner. "Go
ahead, shoot me, Kyle! Shoot me!"

Paws shaking, Enigma shook his head. "You
deserve more than to be shot by me, Ivan! You deserve
to be shot by a Savine!"

I scrambled to my footpaws and held a paw out
towards Enigma. "Enigma, don't! Don't listen to him!
He's just taunting you!"

Ivan's tail flicked irately. "Who are you going to
listen to? Me, the one who knew your father or Scarlet
Savine who doesn't even know your real name?"

Enigma looked frantically from me to Ivan, his
lower jaw moving but no sound coming out. A pleading
look came into my eyes.

"Enigma, don't...please...don't...this is just what he
wants! Can't you see that? He wants to tear us apart!
Ivan wants us to turn on each other! If you kill him,
you'll just be doing him a favor!"

Ivan stiffened slightly, but kept his eyes fixed on Enigma. "She's crazy, Kyle! She doesn't know you like I do!"

The gun lowered a bit as Enigma got a curious look on his face. "What do you mean?"

Biting my lower lip, I looked around for something to hit Ivan in the back of his head.

"I know your life story, Kyle. I know all about you. I *know* you," Ivan continued on, smiling ever so slightly. "Your father died when you were just a pup. Your mother left you all alone. Then, a grey fox took you into his house and showed you to his wife. The wife instantly fell in love with you and, even though she already had two young kits to take care of, she took you in and cared for you. They named you Kyle. When you were a bit older, the mother now had five kits. The father separated you from the rest of his family and took you to his headquarters, P.U.G. As you grew up, he slowly let you become in charge of things and when he thought you were ready, he retired. The fox hoped that his daughter, Scarlet, would follow in his paw prints."

I froze, my heart racing. "My father? He...he knew about P.A.W.?"

Ivan glanced over his shoulders. "Da."

Enigma's chest rose and fell quickly with his breathing. "What happened to my father? How did he die?"

Ivan laughed hollowly, a chilling sound. "I will kill you as I killed him!"

With an angry howl that seemed to shake the building, Enigma was only a blur as he hurled himself at the wolverine. Ripping and tearing at the gigantic creature, the grey wolf bit rapidly at Ivan. A huge black paw with long fur slashed out and hit Enigma in the ribs. With a yelp of anguish, Enigma fell to the floor. Rising over the grey wolf like a leopard preparing to finish off his kill, Ivan paused to let out one of his chilling laughs.

"You're going to die like the we-" he began, but he never finished.

Picking up the pistol Enigma had dropped, I pointed it at the wolverine and fired. Once. Twice. Three times I shot him in the chest. Gideon and Amos hurriedly dragged Enigma out from under Ivan before the wolverine could fall on him. Landing on his knees with a hard thud, Ivan put a paw to his chest and looked at his own blood like it was something he had never seen before. Then, with a deep sudden growl, Ivan lifted his head and leapt at me. Screaming in surprise, Ivan's heavy body crushed me underneath his weight. Closing my eyes in fear, I waited for the fatal blow. It never came. His body moved slightly, then I was blinded by the light. Soft laughing came from above me. Blinking, I saw Gideon and Amos looming over me.

"Hey, sis! How are you?" Amos said joyfully.

"You mean, besides being crushed to death by a monstrous wolverine? Oh, I'm fine. Just fine!"

Enigma was leaning stiffly against the wall, grimacing. "Oh, yeah, I'm fine guys. Just fine, don't worry about me. I was just clawed in the side, huge gashes pouring blood, that's all."

Offering me a paw, Amos hoisted me up to my footpaws. I shook my head and laughed.

"What a pair we make, eh, *Kyle*?" I asked, tilting my head.

Biting his cheek, Enigma avoided looking at me. "Yeah," he said, dragging the word out, "I was going to tell you about that...my real name is Kyle Baker...not Enigma."

Laughing heartedly, I raised an eyebrow. "I already knew the Kyle bit. Will told me that when I was still an FBI agent. Don't you remember me calling you Kyle?" Walking stiffly towards the elevator, I continued solemnly, "So, my parents sort of adopted you before I or the twins were born, no wonder I don't remember you. That's something new. So is the fact that my father worked for P.U.G."

Following me, Jayden raised a paw. "Uh, Scarlet? Didn't you mess up the elevator?"

"Great! You mean we have to walk down all those stairs?!" Groaning, I slapped my forehead.

Patting me on the back, Gideon smiled mockingly. "Now you know what we went through!"

I smiled back at him. "Okay, okay..."

Looking down, I sniffed a little. Arms wrapped around me suddenly, pulling me close. Stiffening, I whirled around and looked into frosty blue eyes.

"Hey, it's okay, Scarlet. Sasha would've been happy you did what you did. If you hadn't, Enigma would've been killed."

Wrapping my arms around him, I buried my face into his torn shirt. "I miss her, Jayden, I miss her so much!"

"I miss her, too, Scarlet. I'm not saying I don't. Just trust God, He knows what to do," he whispered in my ear.

Tears running down my face, I sniffed again. "It

hurts, Jayden. I can't stop thinking about her!"

Resting his chin between my ears, Jayden held me tightly. "I know it does, Scarlet. Trust me, I know."

Amos had stopped by the door of the stairs, now he turned around and walked back to us.

"Hey, bro, listen...I didn't trust you. I was wrong. You're the best older brother anyone could have," Amos said, looking down at the floor.

Laughing softly, Jayden pulled him into the hug.

"I guess this is a group hug?" I asked, chuckling through my tears.

A tear slipped down Amos's face and fell to the floor, he smiled weakly. "Yeah, I guess it is."

Leaning around the corner of the stairwell, Enigma raised his eyebrows.

"Hey, hate to interrupt this joyful family reunion, but can we get going? Silver and Jake are still waiting for us."

Wiping our tears away quickly, we quickly walked over to him.

"Yeah, sorry," I muttered and slowly descended the steps.

Once in the lobby, I walked over to Penelope. "Hey, Penelope. You might want to get someone to go grab the dead wolverine from the top floor. If you're wondering who killed him, I did. It's no secret. He was trying to kill Kyle and I reacted quickly. It was in self defense, sort of."

The Pomeranian nodded her head slowly, eyes wide. "Uh, sure, yeah, whatever you say, Scarlet."

A deep bark and a yowl stopped me dead in my tracks. Turning around, I saw Lucas and a black cat that looked very familiar getting into an argument. Cocking my head, I walked over to them.

"Lucas, wha-" I began, when the black cat turned to me and her bottom jaw dropped. I narrowed my eyes. "Gem? What are you doing here?"

Clearing her throat, she looked from me to Lucas. "Well, uh…you see, Scarlet, I…uh…"

Lucas rolled his eyes. "She works for Ivan as well."

A sharp intake of breath cut of my words. I started sputtering, trying to think of something to say when Cody walked up.

"Oh, Scarlet! Uh…" he began, when I held up a paw.

"Hold your horses! Gem, *you* worked for Ivan?! How?! When?!"

"Yeah, I work for Ivan. How? I'm a spy. That's

what I do. When? Before you went to Germany," she answered quickly.

"Then, why did you help me find him?!"

"He wanted me to tell you where he was. Ivan really wanted to meet you."

Running a paw through my fur, I shook my head. "I trusted you!"

"Yeah, you trusted me, too," Cody laughed, his entire body shaking.

Glaring at him, my ears flattened against my head. "I don't need any input from you, Cody!"

Lucas narrowed his eyes. "I thought I saw you go up to where Ivan was...he should've killed you."

"Yeah, well, he didn't, O'Meara. I killed him," I growled, clinching my fists.

In shock, all their jaws dropped. "What?!"

Jayden came up from behind me and grabbed my paw. "Come on, Scarlet, let's go!"

Suddenly, Silver ran into the building. "Stop right there, Savine!" Holding up his pistol, he aimed it at me. "Murderer!"

"Silver! What are you doing?!" I snarled at him, looking wildly around and started walking towards him.

Jerking the pistol at me, Silver aimed it at me and

raised his voice. "I said stay where you are!"

By now, it seemed everyone in the building was watching us. I groaned and let my head drop a little.

"Silver, stop playing around! Ivan's dead!"

"Ivan? Who's Ivan? Who else have you killed, Savine?" he asked, hackles rising.

Putting a protective arm in front of me, Jayden watched Silver like a hawk watches his prey.

"Scarlet, something's not right. We need to move, now," the black fox whispered in my ear.

Nodding slowly, I started backing away towards an exit. Silver bristled and cocked the gun.

"I mean it, Savine! I will shoot you! I don't care if we were partners, you killed your sister!"

"Silver, you know that's not true!" I yelled at him, eyes wide.

Now, Peter ran out of the elevator. "Scarlet!"

Sighing in relief, I smiled a little. "Thank goodness! Peter, tell Silver I didn't kill Sasha!"

The grey wolf looked at me with frightened eyes. "I don't know about that! You killed a wolverine just a moment ago!"

Looking frantically about, my back finally touched the exit door. Quickly, Jayden and I ran outside. Enigma laughed, leaning on the car.

"Where were y'all?"

"Enigma, get in the car! Now! Silver and Peter have betrayed us!" Jayden and I yelled at him.

Piling into the car, Enigma sped out of the CIA parking lot. Heart pounding in my chest, I shook my head.

"Why would Silver do that?" I murmured.

Shaking his head, Gideon shrugged. "I don't know."

Rolling my eyes, I glanced at him. "I wasn't talking to you."

This was not how I pictured the ending of the war. This is not what I had hoped for. Why would Silver and Peter do this to me? What did I do? Slamming my paw down on the dashboard, I growled in frustration. Why?

CHAPTER 19

Peter looked at the four creatures in front of him. Silver, Gem, Lucas, and Cody stared back at him, a knowing look on their faces.

"Y'all know what we have to do," Peter said, in a commanding voice.

Nodding, the four smiled. "Yes."

Lucas leaned over to Gem and whispered, "I'm not going to let him hurt Scarlet."

Gem purred contently. "You think I would?"

Peter looked out his office window and tapped his claws on it.

"Find Savine and bring her back to me. Dead or alive."

Silver looked at the older grey wolf with soft eyes, bowing his head in respect, he took a small step forward.

"Give me my assignment, Dad. I'll do anything you

ask of me. I've proven to you that I will," Silver said in a hushed voice, keeping his eyes cast downward.

Reaching a paw out to his son, Peter smiled warmly. "Now that Ivan is out of the way, you will be my right paw. Believe me, son, you will have your chance. But not yet. Cody, go with my son and take him back to the house. Have him study some more."

Nodding his head, Cody followed Silver out the door. Lucas and Gem remained in Peter's office. The grey wolf looked at the two.

"What are y'all still doing? Go! You're dismissed!"

Gem hissed at him, her ears flattening. "I may have done as you asked when Ivan was alive, but don't expect me to now! You're not the boss of me!"

Anger flashed across Peter's face as he took a bold step towards the cat. Stepping between them, Lucas growled at Peter.

"I wouldn't do that, Talon!"

The two dogs stared at each other, muscles tense and hearts racing. Finally, Lucas calmed down slightly.

"You haven't heard the last from us, Talon. We'll be back!"

Backing out the doorway, the black cat and the Rottweiler slid out of Peter's office. Gem looked at

Lucas frantically.

"We need to warn Savine!"

"The only problem is; will she believe us?" Lucas asked, looking down the hall. "Peter will call the FBI, then Savine will be running from both the CIA and them..."

Gem stiffened and leaned on the wall, her breathing rapid. "Poor Scarlet. Once an FBI fox, then a CIA fox...now a rogue fox."

To Be Continued